Eliza's Home

....

A CYPRESS HOLLOW NOVELLA

RACHAEL HERRON

RACHAEL HERRON

Eliza's Home/ Rachael Herron. -- 1st ed.
ISBN 978-1-940785-08-0

For Elizabeth, herself.

CHAPTER ONE

Y ou can make it. You *will* make it," Eliza muttered to the truck, which was rattling out a discouraging *put-putting* noise. It was juddering as if trying to shake water off, and every now and then the engine gave an ominous *thunk*.

The salt-wet wind filled the cab of the truck, and goosebumps rose on her arms, just as they always did when she was moving – when the air would be different tomorrow, and the day after that.

The truck shook again and started to slow. "No, no, don't do this. Come on, truck, you owe me." It was only a year old, a 1944 Model 498T. Eliza was sure it wasn't the engine, not in a vehicle this new.

She should have known that guy had watered his gasoline. It had been too good to be true, the farmhouse on the side of Highway 1 with the hand-lettered sign, "Gas For Sale." He hadn't charged enough for the fuel, and she should have been more suspicious. She'd been in a hurry, though, too distracted to stop and wonder about it. She'd just wanted to get back on the road. He'd given her a frank up-and-down while she took the money from her envelope.

"You married, girl?"

Eliza had ignored him. He didn't need to know her story. Not with the way he was leering.

"'Cause if you wasn't, I'd say stay a spell. You hungry? I shot some quail yesterday, got it on ice. You gotta watch for buckshot, and they're mighty tiny birds to take a load like that, but they're still good. You'd like 'em."

She had thrust the money into his hands and avoided his goodbye shoulder squeeze by twisting sideways. Not even thirty minutes north, with the vast blue ocean on her left and a low line of green hills on her right, the Ford had started making funny sounds.

"Come on, come *on*," Eliza said to the truck, which clearly wasn't listening. She'd only been heading north for seven hours, and she'd been planning on making it at least to the Oregon border by late tonight. Then Washington, and then Canada, Vancouver. Across the border, with her envelope of cash. A new country. A new plan – one that would change and move just as she did. When she tired of Vancouver, she'd work her way east across that vast country, and if she bored of that, she'd head down to New York, a city she'd loved when she'd passed through it once at twenty-two, just out of college. Some place George would never find her. "Come on, just to the next gas station. I'll get someone to empty you out and we'll start again, with nice, fresh, clean fuel."

But the Ford refused to comply, shuddering to a slow crawl and finally coming to a complete stop on the side of the road with a cough and a sigh.

"*Shoot.*" Oh, if she got that farmer in her sights, if he drove by right now, she'd give him what for and *how*. Eliza got out and stood next to the truck for a moment, clenching her hands in fury. She kicked a tire and stubbed her toe.

Then, careful to look both ways across the narrow, two-lane highway even though there wasn't a car in sight, Eliza crossed and then clambered up the low sand dune on the other side.

The ocean stretched out in front of her, as deep a blue as a color could be, as vast as the sky above. The water seemed different here to that in San Diego, and she felt as though she was seeing a real ocean for the first time. Down south, the water was friendly, inviting. When you looked at it, you knew you could swim and swim and then dry off in the sun, sand crusting in the crooks of your elbows and knees. Here the water was rough, telegraphing its frigidity even from a hundred yards away. White caps battled each other, and sandpipers raced at the edges of the white froth, dodging the waves as if they were scared to get their feet wet.

"Damn it!" she yelled at the waves. She waited for someone to chastise her. *Good girls never curse.*

No one spoke. There was no one visible for miles, not to the north where a heavy bank of fog drifted landward, nor to the south, where the ocean curved away and out of sight in a tangled blur of blue-gray.

"Hell!" Still nothing. It felt good, and Eliza's heart lifted for a moment before it came crashing back down to reality. She was here. Alone. Running away again.

So she said the worst thing she could think of. "God-damn!" She followed it with a quick, very satisfying scream of frustration.

Lightning didn't strike. God didn't poke his finger through the thickening fog and strike her dead.

"Jesus on a tent pole, woman! What in Hades is wrong with you?" As a man rose from behind the dune to her right, Eliza screamed even louder, this time in fright.

"Are you dying? Have you been stabbed and I just can't see the blood yet?" The man hurried toward her, his long legs pumping through the drifting sand. "Are you wounded?"

"What are you *doing* there? Why were you hiding? Are you a criminal?" What if he was a rapist? A murderer? Perhaps she *should* have taken that farmer up on his offer of a quail dinner.

The man held his fishing pole aloft. "Sure, most criminals carry fishing gear to throw off their victims. No, I was taking a blamed nap in the sun after managing to catch exactly nothing this morning." He was closer now, only half a dune to go, and he was looking at her as if he thought someone should cart her off to the nearest asylum. "I have this crazy need to check on women screaming their heads off."

"Huh. That's strange. I didn't hear a thing," said Eliza, putting her hands on her waist and facing him squarely. The man raised his eyebrows. They were very nice eyebrows, Eliza couldn't help noticing. Full but well shaped, they framed his brilliant blue eyes. He had the lightest stubble across his wide jaw, as if he'd shaved so early that by now, in the early afternoon, it had already started to grow back. He wore a green work shirt with a paint stain on the right cuff.

As if he knew she was looking at it, he flicked his wrist to turn the cuff around. "If you didn't scream, then I'm afraid I have a moral obligation to go find the woman who did, though by the sound of it, she's probably already dead."

"I wouldn't waste your time, then," Eliza said. "Dead is dead."

He shrugged. "True." Looking back at her truck, he asked, "Walk you back to your vehicle, miss?"

"Speaking of dead," she said.

"Ahhh." He offered his arm, and the strangeness of a man popping up in the dunes and offering to walk her across the highway suddenly struck her as more amusing than alarming.

"Thank you, sir." She took it. His bicep was twice, no, three times the size of George's. A shiver ran through her.

"Joshua Carpenter."

"Eliza," she said.

"Eliza . . ."

9

"Just Eliza." She wouldn't say George's last name. That time in her life was over.

"All right, just Eliza." They were across the road now, and Joshua gestured to the hood. "May I take a look?"

"You may," she said, unlatching the hood. "I think I bought bad gas."

Joshua pointed southward. "Blue farmhouse? About thirty miles back?"

Eliza nodded.

"Yeah. This is right about where the cars usually stall. Did he ask you to marry him?"

"I wasn't that lucky. I just got an offer of buckshot quail."

"I'm not sure how Horace thinks he's going to catch a girl that way, but he keeps pulling the same stunts. I can tow you up to my place and drain the tank. I have real gas in a can, too, enough to get you to Cypress Hollow."

Eliza looked up and down the deserted road. "Tow? With your teeth?"

"Will you wait here?" he asked. "Stupid question. I'll be back. Give me twenty minutes."

And with no more said, the man headed eastward, over the low, grassy hummocks and through a stand of eucalyptus, at which point Eliza lost sight of him.

She sat down on the truck's tailgate with a thump.

Fog was rolling in now as if it meant business. The sky darkened as the sun was hidden, and Eliza realized it was later than she'd thought. It would be full night in a couple of hours. And she had nowhere to go. The only home she knew was behind her. Honey's face flashed into her mind, her sister's eyes dark with anger and disappointed hurt. *Go ahead and run, then. Again.*

Pain clawed at her stomach, warring with the hunger pangs. She had an apple, but she'd been saving it for dinner. If only to make herself feel better, she reached across the seat to touch the envelope of money – the cash she'd so carefully put aside, a dollar at a time, for the last year.

It wasn't there.

"No," she said. "No, no, no!" She crawled across the bench seat, scrabbling at the floorboard. "No."

Five minutes later, she admitted defeat. A short while after getting the gasoline, something white had fluttered in her peripheral vision at the open passenger window, but she'd thought it was just part of the newspaper George had left on the seat.

Her envelope. Her getaway fund.

Gone.

Tears filled her eyes as she crawled out of the truck, but she pushed them aside with a furious hand. She would *not* feel sorry for herself. That never did any good for anyone.

She would figure this out. Just like she'd figured everything else out up until now.

A rumble shook the sand beneath her shoes. It got stronger and louder, and Eliza's heart sunk again. What now?

Around the curve of the road in front of her trundled a tractor. The man named Joshua Carpenter rode high on the seat. He'd run into the country and come back with a huge machine to help her out. He gave a cheery wave, and Eliza sighed. It was all just going to get worse, now. At this point, the best thing she could do was take off, run down the road and hope for a friendly passing car to give her a lift to . . . where? Just as she had no money to pay for this tow, to pay for his gas, she wouldn't have any money if she left on foot.

She scrabbled in the storage compartments of both doors and came up with a single nickel and two pennies. They were cold in her clenched palm.

No money still equaled broke, no matter where her feet were planted.

CHAPTER TWO

A fter Joshua expertly attached the ropes, he towed her half a mile, turning inland at a stony drive. Eliza sat in the driver's seat of the Ford, the window down, her elbow out. It was novel and dizzy-making to be moving but not steering.

The driveway twisted and wound through low-spreading oak trees, as though the road had been constructed around them. A jackrabbit raced its way over a small mound, leaping silently.

Joshua stopped in front of a bright red barn. It looked newly built, and sturdy. Tools – a spade and a hoe – leaned against the outer wall, shined and ready for work. By the time she had climbed out of the truck, he had already collected what he needed, appearing from the darkness of the barn carrying a metal can and a hose.

"Just need to siphon it."

And here she was again. Owing another man for help, and this time completely unable to pay. Eliza rubbed her hands together in sudden nervousness. This man, so sure of himself and the way he moved around the truck, made her think of George. What was George doing now? Was he going crazy trying to find her? Had he gone to Honey's house yet? Of course he had. That would have been the first place he went. And, normally, Eliza *would* have taken refuge at her sister's house. It's what she'd done before.

But not this time.

This time she was gone.

Joshua smiled at her and then leaned forward, putting the loose end of the hose that trailed from her gas tank into his mouth.

"What are you—" It looked as if he were going to suck the gas right out of the tank.

And then, sure enough, Joshua turned and spat a mouthful of gasoline onto the ground. He wiped the back of his hand across his lips as he looked directly at her. "Can't say it tastes good, but it wakes a man up, that's for sure."

His eyes – she'd never seen such a blue. They were the color of the San Diego sky, the sky she'd left behind. "You could have killed yourself doing that."

"A man never died siphoning gasoline unless he stole it from a neighbor with a rifle."

He set the hose down on the ground, and fuel trailed from it into the dirt.

Eliza sighed.

"Now, none of that," Joshua said crisply. "We'll have you up and running again in no time."

Shaking her head, Eliza turned. If tears crept into her eyes, she wouldn't let this stranger see them.

The scenery was a good distraction, anyway. If a person were to plan the perfect place to live, this might just be it, she figured. Low hills spread before them, the road to the barn a rocky track through the perfection. Thick fingers of fog trailed over the hill, looking for all the world like dark, gray cotton balls. She longed, for a ridiculous moment, to dig her fingers into that softness, to pull it apart.

"It's a nice view you have," she said, hoping Joshua wouldn't hear the catch in her throat.

"All right, isn't it?" Joshua's words were simple, but his voice held much more. He loved this land. What must that be like? To belong to land, to own it. To feel confident in it. To know you weren't going anywhere else. To not want to leave.

"So nice," she repeated. "Do you live close by?" Maybe his house was over the next rise, just out of sight. Maybe his wife was there, baking a sweet ham, finishing the rolls, wondering what had kept him so long.

He shrugged and knelt to touch the hose. The fuel was now slowing to a trickle. "Sort of."

An odd answer. "So you live close by, yet far away?"

"Exactly."

That smile of his could do things to a girl. Eliza was glad she was only passing through. And that she was done with men forever.

Well. At least she would be, as soon as she could afford a divorce.

Joshua kicked at a clod of dirt at his feet. His cowboy boots were well worn, just like the jeans that clung to his wide, muscled thighs.

Eliza snapped herself back to attention. He was saying something about building a house . . .

". . . so while I work on that, I've been staying here."

She frowned and gestured to the barn. She must have missed something. "Here?"

"There's a hay loft. It's nice, actually. The horses and cows down below make a kind of built-in heater, and I sleep like the dead."

"While you build your house."

He tipped his cowboy hat back and rubbed the side of his nose. "You got a sec, maybe?"

Eliza looked at her truck. She nodded. "It seems I do."

CHAPTER THREE

The man was ambitious, that was for sure. He'd laid the foundation all by himself, and he had the timber lined up, just south of the house. "Tim Saltman – he owns the mill down the valley – sawed it for me, but I took the logs from this land."

"So you're a woodsman, too." Eliza was impressed.

"I want it all to come from here. This will be my home till I die."

She sat on the wooden steps that led up to where he said the porch would be. Behind them stood a naked floor that looked vulnerable – unsheltered from the expanse of sky overhead. "Kind of funny to have steps to a house that doesn't exist. You'd think these would go in last."

"Then how would we sit on them now?" He sat on the step below her and took off his hat, staring at it as if he'd never seen it before. His hair – sandy blond – was curled at the very tips, and judging by its crookedness, he'd cut it himself. It would be so satisfying to even it up, just a little. Eliza could almost feel the scissors in her hands, could almost hear the snick as the hair fell around his shoulders.

"How do you know you'll live here till you die?"

Joshua lifted his face to the sun and paused. "Last few minutes of warmth. Fog'll be here soon."

His response was fine. Maybe he didn't want to answer that kind of question. She didn't blame him. It was enough to sit here, to hear the soft wind in the eucalyptus. Another jackrabbit sped through the unfenced pasture to their right, a huge orange cat on its heels.

"Where do you want to die?" he asked.

Surprised, she said, "I've never stopped to think about it."

He shrugged. "I guess I just knew it when I saw this place. This is it." His voice was slow, like poured honey.

This man was nothing like impatient George, who only talked about the war and gear shafts and what she should make him for dinner.

"It felt like home, has since I first came up the driveway. I knew I had to buy the land. There wasn't anything here then. No barn – I built that first. I wanted cows, and they needed a home before I did."

Eliza wondered, but would never have asked, where he'd got the money to go into farming. She supposed it wasn't cheap, this buying of land and timber and animals.

As if he'd read her mind, Joshua continued to explain. "My father died a few years back, and I was his only family left. He had a small press in Baltimore, but I didn't get the printing bug. The land called me instead."

He said it as though he had been called by a higher power, in the same way a priest was called to his clergy.

Where was Eliza's calling, then? Why did some people hear the voice, loud and clear, while others just floated from thing to thing, from person to person, never completely fitting in, never entirely at home. She felt a brief burst of jealousy toward this stranger who had his life all figured out.

Joshua stood. "Can I show you where I'm putting the rooms?"

Eliza decided she would humor him – accept the gas she couldn't pay for, promise to send him money when she had it. Oh heavens, she couldn't even imagine what she'd have to do to earn it. At least San Francisco had factories. Back in San Diego, she'd been a riveter in the war – her female co-workers had been essential to the war effort, they'd been told. She'd taken pride in using her strong hands to ream holes in steel and dimple them correctly. But when the men came back, the women had all unceremoniously lost their jobs, without any appreciation, cursory or otherwise.

Surely by now, in a city as large as San Francisco, there would be jobs. She'd find one, even if she had to knock on every door three times. It wouldn't have to be in fabrication. She could clean. Cook. Care for children. Waitress. Anything to put a dollar or two in her pocket – anything so she could take care of herself.

"Here," said Joshua, as he led her to the left across the wooden boards. The floor was new, all spring and sway, nothing above it to hold it down, not even the open sky which spread above. Eliza liked this new open space. A brief image of dancing with Joshua on this huge dance floor came into her thoughts.

She shook her head to clear away that ridiculous notion.

"Here's where I'll put the parlor. See that view down the valley? Isn't it fine? There used to be a house right where this one lies – a wagon stop on the coast road – but it burned down at the turn of the century. I used part of its foundation for the basement. See that wooden rail out there? Completely untouched by the fire – it used to be the hitching post for horses. And women used to wait right here, in the old parlor, while the men took care of their business outside."

Of course. The women always stuck inside.

"And through here," he touched her elbow to lead her through an invisible doorway, "will be the dining room. Small, I know, but this isn't a big ranch – it doesn't need all the formality of a house in town. Over here I'll put the kitchen. Can't you just see it?"

Eliza could see it all, right up until his last description. "The kitchen?"

"Yeah. It's going to be big enough for a table, because sometimes it's just nice to eat your eggs in the kitchen and not have to go to the dining room . . ." He trailed off as he saw her expression. "What?"

Shaking her head, she said, "No, it's nothing."

"Tell me."

Eliza bit the inside of her lip. *Well.* There was no ring on his finger – he didn't have a woman, that much was clear. That meant no woman to walk him through these things. And he was a stranger to her, so it wasn't as though she would hurt his feelings. She pointed out the invisible kitchen window. "That's north, right?"

"It is."

"No woman wants a north-facing window in the kitchen."

"Oh. Why?"

"You've heard how artists like a north-facing window? It's because those receive the least direct sunlight. In a home, the kitchen is a woman's studio – but the difference is, she wants the most sunlight possible. When she's cooking oatmeal in the morning, she wants to be able to see when it hits the boil. In the afternoon, when she's proofing bread, she wants to see how big the bubbles in the dough have risen. A woman wants the sun to slant in and out of the windows, to lay tracks on the floor so she can warm her toes." A blush heated her cheeks. Was this all too presumptuous?

"But with the electricity I'm going to run up here . . ."

Eliza shook her head firmly. "No. Not the same. The kitchen is where a woman lives." Her blush deepened and she cursed herself for it. "Where a wife spends a good deal of each day. You want to make it perfect for her."

"I'm not married," he said.

This man had no need of her advice. "Obviously. And moving the kitchen in your plans across the house would be hugely difficult. I understand." She moved back toward the steps. "Forget I said anything. It will be perfect the way you have it."

"But you're right."

Eliza stopped with a jerk. "Pardon?"

"You're absolutely right. I don't know why I didn't think of it before. I'll move it." His grin was so broad she could have swung from it if she'd tried. "Can I ask you about the shape of the dining room?"

CHAPTER FOUR

Eliza met George while visiting her sister, Honey, in San Diego. She was only ever going to stay a short while. She'd almost run out of the money she'd earned from her last teaching job, so the plan was to settle there for a few months and build up her savings, before hitting the road again. But she had days to go before she left, and she was comfortable staying on Honey's settee. She and Honey had gone to teaching college together, but Honey was the one to settle down – who'd found a teaching job and a teacher husband (Bob, a perfectly nice man) in the same week, who'd had a baby within a year of marriage. Eliza was as proud an aunt as ever had been.

When Eliza held Rosemarie, Honey never failed to say, "You need a baby."

Eliza laughed it off. "A girl needs a man first."

"Well get one, and then have a baby. Straightaway, Eliza, promise me you will. Just because our upbringing—"

"What upbringing?"

Honey ignored her. "Just because ours was rough is no reason to never settle down."

"You know I don't settle. Not on a man, not on a place, not on a job."

"You think travel is all there is? Not everyone gets to go to Europe, Eliza. Most women don't get the choices you do. We all settle eventually." Honey took Rosemarie back and gave her a fierce cuddle. "You will, too, Eliza. Someday."

That very afternoon, Eliza met her future husband. George had nodded to the book she'd been holding, in the small bookshop in town. "*Johnny Tremain*. That one's going to be a classic, I think."

He was tall and thin, with very long arms – arms that looked as if they could reach the top shelf in any house. He wore a suit that was threadbare and well worn, but Eliza could tell the quality of the fabric was good. His eyes were so dark that she could almost see herself reflected back in them.

He stuck out his hand. "George Masterson. Pardon me for intruding upon your quiet reflection, but I really think Ayn Rand will be one of the writers most remembered from the last decade. Your Forbes novel there is fine, but have you read *The Fountainhead*?"

Eliza nodded and replied, "I didn't think much of it, though. She doesn't seem like she'd be much fun at a dinner party." She walked away, wondering if he'd follow.

As she took out her pocketbook to pay at the counter, George came up beside her and stilled her hand with his. "Allow me."

Eliza smiled. "I can pay for my own books, thank you."

"Then let me take you to dinner."

"Why?"

"Because you're beautiful."

"Is that all you look for in a dinner date?"

George smiled. "And because you're intelligent. The two combined are perfection."

Eliza had been flattered in spite of herself. She'd gone out with him that night, and two more nights that week. When he picked her up, George charmed Honey and Bob, dandling Rosemarie expertly, dancing the one-year-old from living room to kitchen.

George had a pleasant laugh, and he could speak knowledgeably about any manner of topics. He was kind to waiters when they ate out, and Eliza enjoyed his kisses at the end of their evenings. He was warm and more than responsive, while still respecting her boundaries.

A week later, he broke out of a heated embrace to say, "Marry me."

"Why?" she asked.

"Because I want you to stay the night. And I don't think anything less than a wedding band will get you to do that."

"I'm twenty-seven years old." An old maid, by all standards.

"And I'm just the luckiest guy in the world that someone didn't catch you before this. Marry me."

"Even though you're shipping out again in less than a month?" It was ridiculous. Why would she even think of doing such a thing?

"You'd be able to stay here in San Diego, in military housing. Near Honey."

To stay. "I don't stay. I told you that. I *warned* you."

"I dare you to stay," he said, wrapping his long arm around her, signaling for another round of drinks from the barman.

Eliza smiled. "Oh, you do?"

"You love a challenge, I can tell. I dare you to stay."

It was, perhaps, the only thing he could have said that would have worked.

She took the ring he offered (small but serious, a gold band and a slip of a diamond) and put it on her third finger.

Honey knew a minister. Eliza and George were married within a week. For their honeymoon, they went to San Luis Obispo and stayed in a huge pink hotel. Their room was styled to look like a grotto, with water trickling down rock walls. In the middle of the night she woke in his arms, worried that a river was rising, that the water she was hearing would drown her.

She wasn't as sad as she should have been when he shipped out. She couldn't tell if it was because she was glad to be alone again, or if she wanted to go, too. To get on a boat and sail for parts unknown, feel the wind in her hair, not know what kind of sky she'd be under tomorrow.

Instead, she was in a tiny white house with clean white walls, cooking herself small dinners in pots that she washed and put away in the same place every night. Her empty suitcase lived under the bed. Sometimes, in the middle of the quiet nights, she'd lie on the rug next to the bed and reach out, resting her fingers on the brass clasp. That was the way she slept best.

CHAPTER FIVE

An hour later, after her tank was totally drained, Joshua poured the gasoline from his metal can into her truck's tank. "That should do you."

"I hate that I can't pay you. I'll mail you the money as soon as I get it." She hadn't explained losing her envelope of money, had just said she was shorter than she would like to be. It wouldn't do to cry in front of this man.

He waved his hand again, as he had the first time she'd brought it up. "Don't need your money."

"But I will send it to you. With interest." She wanted to reach out and shake his hand, to prove her worth, to show she'd keep her word, but she was scared of touching him. This man who wore his love of this land on his sleeve.

Joshua opened the driver's door for her, offering his arm to assist her up.

"I'm fine," she said, hauling herself into the cab. "Used to it." She could sell the truck, she realized. Drive as far as she could – surely this tank would get her to San Francisco? – sell it for cash as fast as she could. That money would put her up in a women's hostel for a little while, at least for long enough to find work. Somewhere.

Friendless.

Alone.

She slowly rolled down the window and allowed herself to stare at Joshua's face for a few seconds. He seemed so . . . open. So kind. It was probably a ruse, though, wasn't it? He was probably just like George.

Joshua stepped forward, leaning his large hand on the frame of the truck's front window. "I've been trying not to ask, but I can't just let you go without knowing. Where are you heading?"

"San Francisco. Probably." Farther when she got the money.

"What will you do there?"

Eliza sat straighter. "Anything. I can do anything."

One eyebrow rose. "Yeah?"

"I can use a pop rivet gun. I can paint a house. I can drive a cable car – I read somewhere they have one woman doing that already. I can drive a forklift at the docks." She realized what she was really trying to say. "I can do anything a man can do. If they'll let me. I guess that will be the biggest problem."

Joshua took a deep breath. "Can you hammer a nail?"

Surprised, she said, "Yes."

"Can you lift fifty pounds?"

"I'm strong," she said, knowing it was true. "I work as hard as any man."

"Can you make sure a plumb line is true?"

"One of my best qualities. Plumb lines." She barely knew what one was.

"Do you want a job?" he asked.

"Yes," Eliza said.

CHAPTER SIX

Honey said, "You have to remember, you're a Navy wife now."

Eliza flopped backward onto her niece Rosemarie's small bed. "Those words don't even make *sense* to me. A Navy wife? I don't know how to be one of those. The other wives on base won't even talk to me, did you know that? When I shop at the commissary, they get all quiet and stare at me."

"Do you even *try*?"

"No," said Eliza. "I shouldn't have to try."

When she wrote letters to George, who was still away at sea, she didn't know what to say. What did he want to know? She couldn't be sure (doubted, in fact) that he was getting any of the letters she sent anyway. She didn't *know* him well enough to know what he wanted to hear about. Did he love hearing about the turning of the season, and how the sycamores were changing color? Did he want to hear the gossip Honey gleaned at church?

Did he want to know that she'd failed at finding a teaching job? Would he mind that instead she was working as a riveter? He'd told her flat-out before he left that he didn't want any wife of his working at all, and it had turned into the only fight they'd had in the three weeks they'd been together. Once he was gone, she'd chosen to ignore his wishes. He couldn't have been serious, could he? George couldn't really expect her to sit in a closed room, just waiting for his return.

And it had been exciting, taking the job. Getting her blues to wear, pulling her hair back, making sure her nails were short enough that her hand fit inside the PBY's narrow wing blade. She loved the feeling of the rivet gun in her hand, placing its drive shaft against the shank, actuating the hammer with the rivet set. She was good at it, and the noise and smell of metal on metal pleased her. The other girls were great, too, and she had formed a fast bond with six of them – they went everywhere together when they weren't working. They'd already got a reputation in downtown San Diego as the Loud Girls, the ones who whooped and hollered until much too late into the night. Josephine was her favorite, and the fastest of their lot. One night she'd taken Eliza to a bar near the marina, and when the sailors had come in, Josephine had simply chosen the most handsome one and taken him home with her. Home! With her! The next day at work, she'd apologized for leaving Eliza behind. "But he was too good to waste, honey. I had to get him before anyone else did," she'd explained.

Honey yanked the towel Eliza was folding out of her hands and refolded it. "That's ridiculous. You have to try to make friends with them."

"I can't belong to their little club. I don't even *look* like them. Their hair is always all . . ."

"Done?" Honey reached out and tugged one of Eliza's long, messy locks. "Whereas yours is up in a kerchief most of the time."

"That's how we wear it at work."

"But do you have to wear it like that when you're not there? A few bobby pins and I could . . ."

Eliza swatted away her hand. "I might not stay."

"For dinner?"

That wasn't what she had meant – but she didn't admit it. "A couple of girls are meeting downtown, and I..."

Honey sighed. "Go, then. You always do."

***

Joshua had been right – it was cozy in the barn's loft. Hearing the soft noises of the animals below warmed Eliza as she made the small bed. She couldn't wait to pull the dark woolen blanket around her, raising the thick red quilt with it. She'd be toasty. And safe.

She came down the ladder with care, glad she'd brought her work jeans with her. They'd come in handy here, more so than this dadgummed skirt.

Joshua had finished moving himself out to the small shed and was watering the animals.

Eliza said, "Are you sure you'll be all right out there? Won't it be cold? Or too small?"

"The shed's just got tools in it now. Plenty of room for a rucksack. And I don't get cold easily."

"But I'm taking your bed." Again, Eliza stupidly blushed. She didn't want to analyze the response she was having to the kindness of this man. She was only taking a job. That was all.

"Just a bed. Gotta sleep somewhere, right? I'm just sorry I don't have a more official place for you to stay. Are you sure you don't mind? Because Mrs. Stillwell over in town rents a room and I could . . ."

"And have to talk to people?" Eliza smiled. "I'd much rather be out here, away from all that."

"About that," said Joshua, not meeting her eyes. He tested the strength of a board in the barn wall by pushing on it, as if the endurance of the wood were the only thing that mattered. "People will talk."

"I know. I guess that's more your problem than mine."

"How do you figure?"

Eliza reached over a stall door to touch the muzzle of an older mare. It huffed against her palm and she smiled. "No one knows me here. I'm an itinerant worker, just passing through. A divorcée." The new word felt strange in her mouth. "You're the one with the reputation to lose. You're the one who lives here."

Joshua shrugged and smiled. "I don't care."

But *they* would care. Eliza knew everyone in the closest town, Cypress Hollow – everyone for a thirty-mile radius, for that matter – would care. "We'll see, I suppose."

"A divorcée, you said?"

Eliza focused on the scratchy velvet of the horse's lips. "Not quite yet. But I will be soon."

"What happened?"

Eliza silently gripped the wood of the stall's door.

"Never mind," Joshua stuttered. "None of my business. We'll start the framing tomorrow. Good night to you."

The words were tumbling out of her mouth before she could stop them. "I might not be here in the morning." She couldn't guarantee she wouldn't run. She couldn't trust herself not to, after all. He should be warned. It was only fair.

"That's fine, but I hope you will be." A brief smile, and he was gone.

CHAPTER SEVEN

George shipped out in 1942. By Christmas in 1943, with him still away, Eliza had gone against his wishes and moved in with her sister, leaving their little house unoccupied.

"I can't live near those sad, sad women for another minute," she'd written him. "Not when I'm so close to Honey. All they do is talk about their husbands and when they might come home. And gossip," she wrote, as though the girls she worked with didn't gossip – they lived for the latest dirt. But that was different. "It isn't right."

"I want you to keep my house for me," wrote George. "As my wife."

He didn't actually write, *It's your duty,* but Eliza heard the words. And she moved out anyway.

When he came home, she met the ship at port. She watched every man disembark with a jolt of surprise. Could that be him? Or that one? Did she have any idea who she'd married? What was she doing? Who had she become?

Josephine stood next to her. A sailor she'd been corresponding with was on the same ship. She squeezed Eliza's arm. "Aren't you excited, darlin'? Gonna see your man tonight? A little roll in the marital hay?"

Eliza shrugged off her touch. "I don't know."

"You don't *know*? The only reason I don't have sex every night is 'cause sometimes I need my beauty sleep."

Eliza's temper snapped. "You can't just talk like that, Josephine," she hissed. "Women don't *do* that. It's not *right.*"

Josephine looked as startled as if she'd slapped her. "You don't judge me. I love that you've never judged me, like all the rest."

"Yeah, well, maybe I was wrong."

"Don't take your nervousness at seeing the husband you know nothing about out on me, Eliza. It's not my fault you strapped yourself to someone for life."

Eliza sighed and scanned more men's faces. "Not strapped," she said.

"What?" said Josephine over a ship horn's blare.

"Trapped," Eliza said quietly.

Josephine squeezed her shoulder, kissed her cheek, and ran forward to meet the man she'd been looking for.

Despite her fears, when George swung into sight, Eliza knew him immediately. He wrapped his long arms around her and kissed her full on the mouth, coming up for air with a shout of pleasure. "Let's go home, sugar. I want to show you how much I missed you."

Eliza nodded and smiled, pushing down the emotion she didn't dare name, shoving it back down into her chest where she could hide it for as long as she needed. Forever, if it came to that. Which it probably would.

CHAPTER EIGHT

A week after Joshua gave her the job, Eliza was surprised to find herself still in the barn's loft. The road hadn't called to her with its siren song of flight. Not yet. So she would stay a little longer. She'd stay as long as she wanted to, but not a minute more.

Ten days after she'd arrived, the blisters on her palms turning to calluses, the ache in her neck and shoulders finally dulling, Eliza drove herself to Cypress Hollow for the first time.

It was a sweet town, she had to admit. Only a few rows of low-slung houses, it was set back from the ocean with Main Street running along the edge of the beach, turning northeast as the coast curved. At one end stood a lighthouse, painted blindingly white. At the other, a new-looking gazebo perched proudly on a spit of grass. Red and white bunting from the last celebration still hung from its rafters. Cypress Hollow was the kind of town one could drive through without a glance. There wasn't even a stop sign, just the single curve to slow down drivers.

Eliza picked up thread from the general store – she'd already torn a hole in her jeans kneeling on a splintered board. She bought flour, milk, and meat – she'd tried to unofficially take over the cooking from Joshua, but he'd had none of it, declaring his love of the kitchen, even one standing under the stars. His stews were hearty, and he made the best chicken pot pie she'd ever tasted. At the front counter of the small shop, a woman with a kind face took her money and said, "I'm Annie. You're staying out with Joshua Carpenter, right?"

"Right." Eliza wanted to add, *I'm working there. Only working. It's not what you think.* But she didn't. She shouldn't have to.

"Welcome to town," was all the woman said.

As Eliza walked the short blocks lined with small shops, she passed Tillie's Diner. The unmistakable smell of bacon wafted out the open door, and she entered with only a slight hesitation to her step. The diner was a long room lined with glass windows that looked across the street to the dunes. It had a row of red booths and a long glossy counter lined by stools. A young man stood at the till, wiping its surface with a clean white towel.

"Anywhere you like," he said.

She took a booth, enjoying the way the leather crumpled against her knees. The man, obviously the owner, brought her a cup of coffee without asking. "I'm Bill," he said. "You're the new gal up at Carpenter's ranch."

"I am." Again, she would make no apology. No explanation.

But it seemed as if he didn't need one, either. "Good man," said Bill. "Glad he's got some help with that house. He was in here yesterday. Said you're a good worker."

Eliza felt herself flush with pleasure. She *was* a good worker. And she'd never worked so hard in her life, nor had she ever slept so deeply at night. "I like it."

The woman at the booth behind her turned her head to join the conversation. "What do you like about it?" She wore a jaunty yellow, knitted beret and had deep brown eyes sunk like two raisins pressed into her face. She was of indeterminate age – the wrinkles on her face could have been caused by either time or the sun.

Startled, Eliza took a moment to think her answer through. "I like the sanding the best."

"Unequivocal, isn't it?"

That was it exactly. Once you sanded something smooth, it was smooth. No going back to its rough beginning.

"I like knitting myself," the woman said, holding up a flash of red yarn before returning it to her lap. "If you make a mess of it, you can take it all apart. Not so with wood."

"Not so," agreed Eliza.

"How about you?"

"Pardon?" Eliza had lost track of the conversation already.

"You knit?"

"No," she said. Honey did, and Eliza had always meant to learn, but hadn't yet. She'd always put it off for another day.

"Oh, you should. Can I sit with you? I'm Bertha Crossley."

"Eliza," she said.

"All right, Eliza. Let me show you what I'm doing. You look like you'll be a good knitter." Bertha swung herself into the other side of the booth. "Take these needles. I always have a spare set on me, for emergencies such as these."

Eliza liked being considered an emergency. And over the most perfect bacon she'd ever had, chased by the darkest coffee, Eliza learned how to cast on and how to do the knit stitch. It wasn't as easy as Bertha made it look. Not half as easy. As yet another stitch raced away from her, jumping off the needle to its death, Eliza cursed. "*Damn.* Oh. I'm sorry."

"Cuss away, darlin'. Sometimes it's just what the knitting needs to hear."

"You make it look so easy," said Eliza with despair. "And it's not. I'm so clumsy. Wooden things are far easier."

"But can you bring the sawhorse to bed? Sawdust in bed is itchy. Knitting can always be with you, tucked under your pillow if need be. Wherever you go."

Eliza considered this as Bertha fixed the mess she'd just made with nimble fingers. "Wherever I go." That sounded nice. "I do like to go places." She pictured herself on a train, knitting between her fingers. Where would she arrive when the train stopped? New York? New Orleans?

She thought of Joshua in his snug home. Unmoving.

"Where *will* you go, Eliza?"

"I don't know," she said honestly. "I was headed north when I ran out of money. When Joshua offered me the job."

Bertha shrugged and joined a piece of blue yarn to the striped scarf she was making. It was magical, the way the stitches seemed to trickle right out of her fingers. "You could just stay."

Smiling, Eliza said, "I couldn't."

"Why not?"

"Because I was going . . . somewhere else."

"Why?"

"I was . . ."

"Running away?"

Eliza focused on a single stitch that had suddenly multiplied into two. "I was just going."

"'Scuse me for not believing you. You've got that running look, dearie. A man, huh?"

Eliza gave one nod.

"Husband?"

Another nod.

"Hit you?"

One more nod.

Bertha put her hand over Eliza's, stilling the work. "Good for you. A man who clobbers a woman deserves to be horse-whipped but seldom is. You've run to a good place, is all I'm saying. Joshua Carpenter is a good man."

"We're not . . . we're not involved."

Bertha smiled. "Of course not. Now, don't forget to drop the leg of the stitch. That's how you're getting those extra stitches."

CHAPTER NINE

The first time George hit Eliza, he said it was an accident.

"Jesus. You were in my way. That's all." Then he changed his story. "I thought I was back on the ship, and I overreacted. I shouldn't have done that."

Holding her cheek, not daring to look at the pan she'd burned, she wondered if that's how he would have reacted to a man. With a slap to the cheek? Was that really how men on the ships fought?

That night, she waited until his breathing was heavy before slipping out from under his arm to lie on the rug next to the bed. She slept with her fingertips on her suitcase, carefully rising before he did, so he wouldn't know.

Then Eliza made him breakfast in their tiny jail of a kitchen. He got one freebie, she decided. One fluke, one gigantic mistake. She was in this to *stay*, and she'd give him that much.

The second time, George hit her as if she were a man. A solid upper-cut to the jaw flung her backward, striking her head on the mantel. She came to in his arms, George holding a bloody towel to her hair. She heard it then, over the sound of his sobs – the solid *chunk* the brass latch of her suitcase made when she shut it, and she knew, even then, that she was grateful to him. He'd unlocked the padlock for her, the one she thought she might never find the key for. He'd made it simple.

***

The days at Joshua's ranch took on a pattern. In the morning, he lit a fire in the fire pit. She used an iron pan blackened by flame to cook him four eggs, scrambled. He swore he'd never had a better egg in all his life, and while Eliza didn't believe him – they were only scrambled, after all – she let herself bask in the tone of his voice when he said it.

Then they worked, and they worked hard. Joshua didn't seem to treat her any differently to a male worker, asking her to carry exactly as heavy a load as he did. If he carried lighter loads to make up for this, he didn't let on. They worked the same hours, and at the end of the day they sat at the picnic table Joshua had made, in what would be the house's backyard someday. Everything they ate they cooked over the fire Joshua built back up from the morning's coals. Eliza made "cowboy coffee" the way Joshua had showed her, pushing the boiling grounds in the percolator down with a blast of cold water from the well.

Sitting under the sycamore, they watched the sun drop behind the hill every night. Sometimes the fog created a sunset that rang false with its sheer extravagance, and other nights the sky was so clear that one second the sun was there and the next second, gone. Even though her hands still hurt every night, even though she could count on digging out at least three splinters before doing the dishes in the back creek, she knitted as the sun went down.

"That's looking good," Joshua said one night, gesturing at her scarf.

"You're too kind. It looks like a dog's breakfast."

He reached out with one finger and then drew it back before touching the work. "Sorry. It just looks . . . soft."

"It is. Bertha gave me the yarn. She spun it herself, which gives me nightmares that I'm going to waste it all and she'll never speak to me again."

"Are we talking about Bertha Crossley? Because if so, you'll have to run away in the dark of night to escape her friendship."

Another stitch raced toward the hem. At this rate, the simple brown scarf would look like lace by the end of it, albeit unintentionally so. "Damn," she whispered.

"But I hope you won't." Joshua's voice sounded different and Eliza looked up sharply.

"What?"

"Run away in the dark of night."

"Oh." Eliza's stomach flipped, as sometimes it did when she caught sight of him unexpectedly while they were working. Two days ago, they'd had a surprise heat wave, and he'd stripped off his shirt while up on the new roof. Eliza had glanced up at him once, gawping at his muscles flexing while he wielded his hammer, and at the sweat glistening between his shoulder blades, and then she'd made herself hurry away, back to her own saw-horse. He'd put his shirt on by the time he came down again but the image of his bare chest was already burned into the backs of her eyes.

"You did that once, after all."

"What?"

"You've never told me about your last great escape."

She hadn't. He hadn't asked.

"What was he like, your husband?"

Eliza's fingers stilled. She carefully placed the knitting in her lap and reached for her porcelain coffee cup. Joshua always let her have it, keeping the old tin cup for himself.

"He was . . . he just wasn't quite as good as I thought he was. He didn't live up to his potential."

"He was a jerk, is what you're saying."

Eliza nodded. "I didn't know it when I married him, of course. The war had just started, and I thought I knew what I was doing. I'd been around the world already, or at least to me it felt like I had. I'd got my degree, paid for every penny of it by working two jobs. I'd taught English in Turkey."

Joshua blinked. "I've never been outside the dark black line on the map of the States." His eyes darkened. "Except for the war."

Of course. Always the war.

Eliza touched her knitting lightly. "But you knew you wanted to be here, right where we are now."

"As soon as I got back, I knew I'd never leave."

"I didn't know where I was meant to be. I went to Scandinavia and ate reindeer. I danced in a Venetian *osteria*. I taught English wherever I went, getting tutoring jobs by word of mouth. I was good at it, but it wasn't enough. I was always travelling to somewhere. I just never knew where that was."

"You still don't?" Joshua kept his eyes carefully toward his tin cup.

Eliza shook her head. "Still looking."

"How did you end up stateside again?"

"It was 1938, and the talk was getting scary. No matter where I went, no matter which train I took, people were talking about Germany. I didn't understand exactly what they meant, but I knew from the way I overheard people talking that the situation was getting more heated. In a café, a man told me that they'd taken his employer's family the night before, all of them. They were just gone." Eliza paused, touching the surface of the picnic table. It should have been rough – it was just for eating outside, after all. But Joshua had taken the time to sand it so smooth it felt like fabric under her fingertips. "So I took a boat back."

"You've been so far." Joshua's voice was full of marvel. "What was the best part?"

"New York," said Eliza without hesitation. "You should see the streets there at Christmas. There's nothing like those lights shining against the snow. The shops, all lit up and decorated, it's like every place sells sparkle and warmth and happiness, even if it just sells hats. I'd love to go back there and see it in spring or summer." She thought. "And Seattle was a surprise. It always smelled kind of like a dog that went for a swim in the ocean, and I liked the way the sidewalks felt under my feet, rising and falling on their way to the water. And San Diego." Her voice trailed off.

"That's where you were living? With your husband?"

Eliza nodded.

"Huh. Where did he go?"

Eliza didn't have to ask what he meant. "The Pacific. Saipan and Tinian."

He inclined his head. "Rough out there."

They'd never talked about it, though of course Eliza had wondered. "You were . . ."

"In Europe. France. I flew."

Simple words that meant so much more. "I can't imagine what you've seen."

He gave her a sideways glance. "Maybe you can."

"Maybe."

They sat in silence for a moment. Then she said, "I worked while he was away."

"Teaching?"

"No one wanted me for that. Not in San Diego, anyway. There were enough teachers there, and with the boys gone, not enough hands to work in the Consolidated Vultee plant. I applied to be a riveter on a dare from a friend. She never thought I'd do it, but I loved it."

"Jigs and pins."

"Yep." She straightened her spine and could almost feel the rivet holes under her fingertips. "Clamps and fasteners. I was good at it. I've always been good with my hands." Picking up her knitting, she examined the holes in the fabric. "Well, usually I am. Maybe not this time."

"That's looking good, Eliza."

The way he said her name . . . Eliza was suddenly as nervous as if he'd reached out and touched her. She stood. "It's late. I'll wash the dishes."

"Leave 'em. I'll get them later."

On other nights she'd protested. If he cooked, she made sure she cleaned up afterward. But not tonight. There was something different in the air, something that mattered too much. "Thank you. Good night."

"Good night, Eliza."

"I might not be here in the morning." She might not. She might repack her suitcase at three in the morning, pin her money into her blouse (because she would not lose it again), and hit the road. You never knew.

He always said the same thing. "That's fine, but I hope you will be."

CHAPTER TEN

Eliza had to wait until the bruising went down to leave. She knew questions would arise, a single woman driving a long way on her own – the same questions always came up. *You married? Where're your kids? Where are you going? With no plan at all?* She would draw less speculation if she didn't have a black and blue jaw. It was easier than she thought it would be to wait – George was strangely compassionate toward her, sweet and loving, as though he really meant it. And maybe he did. She understood then what she'd never understood before. She knew why women stayed with the men who hurt them. It was easy when you felt so loved, when the man who'd hurt you was spending all his considerable energy making you feel safe and secure. You knew he'd kill any other man who touched you the wrong way. The word "irony" rattled in Eliza's head.

When she'd healed, when her face looked normal and was back to the right shape and color, she packed her suitcase. Just the suitcase, that was all. It was all she'd had at one time, and it had been enough. Everything else she left behind. The radio they'd picked out together, the red curtains she'd sewed, the potted plants in the post-age-stamp-sized backyard. Even the pots and pans she'd been so proud of were left in the kitchen. Eliza was a person who ran, and runners go faster when they run light.

She didn't care that George would be hurt by her leaving. That was what he got. But Honey . . . she was a different story.

"So," said Honey, seeing the suitcase on the floorboards of the truck. "You're giving up."

"I'm not—"

"You're not going to try to stick it out. For me."

Eliza held out her hand, but Honey was distracted by Rosemarie running into her knees. She knelt to hug the child and didn't meet Eliza's eyes. "I thought we were worth it to you."

You were. You are. But nothing was worth staying with George for. She hadn't wanted to have to tell Honey, but who was she kidding? "He hit me."

"So?"

Eliza couldn't hide the shock in her voice. "So? We grew up with *nothing.* How many times were we whipped at the orphanage? Don't you think I deserve more than that? More than just being a good wife? Accepting that sort of treatment? You'd expect me to stay at his side?"

"I stay," said Honey flatly.

The despair Eliza felt in the pit of her stomach was a wide, gaping wound. "No. Honey, no." She struggled to breathe around the sudden grief. "*Come with me.* You and Rosemarie. Leave Bob. We'll fit in the truck. We never have to come back."

Honey sighed as if this was a conversation they'd had a million times. "You don't get it. It's a choice. Everyone settles, Eliza. Everyone. Someday you will too." She smiled, but it didn't reach her eyes. "The sun is prettiest through the rain, right? That's what you always said when we were children."

Eliza reached out her hand. "Please, Honey."

Honey shook her head and left the room, Rosemarie held tight in her arms. Over her shoulder, she said, "I'm a *good* mother."

As if Eliza had ever asserted anything else. It hurt more than George's fist ever could.

CHAPTER ELEVEN

Every morning, Joshua left her a pitcher of water just outside the barn door. She suspected him of warming it over the campfire, because some mornings it wasn't half as cold as it had every right to be. It was pleasant to wash herself in the half-light that trickled through the knotholes. Once a week, Eliza went to the well and pumped enough frigid water over her head to wash her hair. She'd almost forgotten what hot running water felt like.

She barely missed it.

Six weeks had passed. Every night Eliza said the same words to him. Every night he echoed his hope she'd still be there the next day.

And every morning, she woke in the little nest Joshua had made of the upper loft. And when she heard his two horses blowing air and pawing the hay below her, when she rolled over and wrapped the old quilt more tightly around her body, she felt the same two things.

Terror.

Elation.

Both things fit into the same wide spot in the middle of her chest.

Now that the house was framed, the wiring and plumbing finished, they were working on the kitchen. Last week they'd built the counters, and yesterday Joshua had fired up the new stove for the first time.

"Bacon over there. And I cooked you an egg."

She'd thought she'd risen early today, the sun barely clearing the eastern hill, but apparently not.

"How's that worm?" asked Eliza, sitting on floor-boards she'd sanded by hand – working until blisters formed at the very tips of her fingers, which had made her nightly knitting difficult for a few days.

"What?"

"The one you must have caught this morning."

"Oh, that one." He flashed a grin at her. "Tasted good with the bacon. Say, I know we haven't put in the glass yet, so I'm jumping the gun, but what kind of curtains do you put in kitchen windows?"

With that much space, with that much light . . . "Sheer white. Just imagine, the windows open, this same breeze blowing through here." It smelled wonderful in the naked room, like coffee and sawdust.

He nodded. "That's what I was thinking. It's been nice, cooking every meal outside, but at some point it's going to rain. Having a roof over the stove is good."

Rain. Fall was coming. Where would she be when the heavens started opening? Not here, surely. Joshua would be done with the house, and she'd be out of a job again. She'd have more money in her pocket, and she'd be able to get back on the road, the wind in her hair the way she loved it . . .

What a strange feeling, this disappointment coursing through her.

Joshua picked his measuring tape up and folded it, the bends in the fabric worn and precise. He slipped it into his pocket, where it always sat.

"You're careful with all your tools."

He looked down at his hands. "Of course. They're important to me."

Eliza felt a warmth in her stomach and a question rang in her head . . . a very dangerous question. "Why didn't you ever marry?" The words were out of her mouth before she could stop them.

"I never met the girl who could stand me."

"That's ridiculous. You're . . ." Joshua was the sweetest, kindest, funniest . . . "Tell me something true."

He pulled the tape back out of his pocket and unfolded it again and measured the raw edge of the counter, where they still needed to install the doors. He kept his eyes carefully on the tape, as if he thought its length might change if he looked away.

"Still seventeen inches?" Eliza said. She stood, slowly. She was so close to him, just a few feet away.

"Oh, woman." Joshua rubbed the edge as if he could sand it with his fingertips.

The tension between their bodies was almost tangible. She could practically see it, vibrating and taut. Eliza felt that blast of elation again. For one long second, she thought about standing and wrapping her arms around his neck. Touching his skin. What would his body feel like against hers?

But he'd never been anything but nice. Never anything but a good employer. Considerate. Professional.

Blast it *all*.

Joshua said, "To answer you, I was engaged once, but the girl wanted a house in town."

"You broke up over the position of a house?"

"Kind of tells you what I was worth."

A girl let him go over a house? This man? With those eyes that reminded her of blue ice, melting with earnest, deliberate kindness?

"I'm going to town," Eliza said, making up her mind at that moment, needing to get away. "Do you need anything?"

Looking surprised, he shook his head. "Well . . . if you could get another bag of penny nails . . ."

Eliza gave a brief nod and was gone, only remembering the egg he'd made her when her wheels hit paved road.

CHAPTER TWELVE

As she drove into town, rolling down the window didn't help her sort out the tangles in her brain. She touched the knitting on the seat next to her in the same way she used to touch her suitcase's clasp.

Bertha. She had to find Bertha.

She wasn't at Tillie's. She wasn't at the market, or the post office, or the small town library. Bertha was so rarely at home – *no time for it*, she'd say, *got too many other places to be* – that her house was the last place Eliza tried.

The curtains were drawn, even though it was now past nine. No one answered Eliza's knock, and when she pushed the door open, the silence that met her was strangely thick.

"Bertha?" she called. "It's me, Eliza. Are you home? May I come in?"

"Who is it?"

"Eliza," she repeated. "Are you all right?" She went down the dark hallway to the first open door.

"I'm fine," said Bertha in a small voice, which worried Eliza – usually Bertha was as quiet as a freight train. She was sitting under a green knitted afghan and looked small propped up against her pillows.

Eliza hurried to her. "Are you sick? Do you need a doctor?"

"No doctor for what I've got."

"What? What is it?" She sat on the edge of the bed.

Bertha smiled. "Really, child. It's no worry. I'm just busy being sad today. As long as you're here, though, can you get me my knitting basket from the parlor?"

"Of course. And a cup of tea," said Eliza firmly. "I'll be right back."

Tea at hand, served with a homemade banana muffin from the kitchen, Eliza settled at the foot of Bertha's bed. A ray of sunlight came through the open curtains and warmed Eliza's back.

Bertha smiled thinly. "You look like a cat, all tucked up there."

"I love a good puddle of sunshine," said Eliza, holding her knitting gently. "Now, eat a bite of your muffin. That's good. Tell me about the sadness."

"You're not usually this bossy."

"I've never had to be with you."

Bertha carefully wrapped the yarn around her needle. "Every year, on this day, I stay in bed and cry."

"Why this particular day?"

"My husband Nathaniel died on it. Twelve years ago."

On a previous visit to Bertha's, Eliza had seen Nathaniel's picture, hung on the parlor wall in a place of honor. "You talk about everything, and everyone else. But never about him."

Bertha inclined her head.

"Why?"

"Because it still hurts too much."

Eliza spoke slowly, measuring her words. This felt important – she needed to get it right. "You were happy together. Will you tell me about that?"

"What do you mean? What more can I say? We were happy. What more do you want me to say?" Bertha stabbed at the shawl she was making.

"I don't know if I believe in true love. True happiness."

"It exists," Bertha said crossly. "That I know."

Eliza leaned forward and kept her eyes on Bertha's. "Then tell me about it."

With a sigh, Bertha set the shawl down. She closed her eyes. "I don't talk about him because if I do, I might get something wrong. And if I get something wrong, I might start to believe it myself, and then what I know about him won't be true anymore." She stopped speaking.

Eliza waited a beat and then said, "Tell me anyway. Trust yourself."

Bertha's eyes slowly opened, and she picked up the shawl again. She knitted almost a whole row. Eliza let the silence settle between them.

Finally Bertha said, "People talk about their perfect love being their other half. The piece that makes them whole. Nathaniel and I were never like that. We were oil and water. He liked things quiet and orderly and tidy. I liked things loud and messy. I wanted to *live*. He wanted peace. When he ate an apple, he had a procedure, a formula that he had to follow every time."

"What was the formula?"

Bertha smiled, her face suddenly as bright as the sunlight that bathed her cheeks. "He'd wash it twice and would only dry it on a tea-towel I hadn't yet used. He didn't mind germs, he just didn't like the taste of dust, he always said. Then he'd twist the stem off, going through the alphabet. A, B, C, no matter when the stem came off, he'd go back to B. "B is for Bertha," he'd say. Then he'd get out his pocketknife – only that would do, none of *my* knives could possibly be sharp enough – and he'd divide it into eight equal pieces and cut out the pips. He ate each piece one after another, chasing each slice with three huge gulps of milk. Every afternoon, he did this, every afternoon at three o'clock sharp. Didn't matter if I'd got lunch on the table late that day, if we'd just finished eating an hour earlier. He wanted his apple at three, and nothing else would do."

"What about when apples weren't in season?"

Bertha laughed. "You don't even want to know what he would do to an orange."

"Was he particular about everything?"

Tilting her head to the side, Bertha said, "You would think. You'd think he'd want me to keep the house in a certain way, wouldn't you? But no. No matter what I wore, whether it was my Sunday best or my cleaning housedress, he said I was the prettiest thing he ever saw. If I burned the roast, he said the char was tasty. Once I put a cup of salt into a batch of his favorite blueberry muffins instead of sugar. I don't like blueberries, so I didn't try one. Wasn't till I fed one of that batch to a neighbor that I learned what I'd done – he'd been choking them down for days. He would have died before criticizing me." Her words dropped as slowly, in time with the stitches that slipped from one needle to the other. "He *could* have criticized me, you know. Everyone does. It's what marriage is about – getting irritated, and then forgiving what made you that way. Loving anyway. That's what I was always doing to him. Forgiving him for his errors. He just never seemed to hold anything against me."

"That sounds wonderful."

"You'd think so, wouldn't you? Sometimes I'd get so mad at that man. I wanted to rile him! To make him lose control! To make him use a different goldurn knife to cut his dadgummed apple. Once I pretended I forgot his birthday. All day, I felt terrible, but I wanted to see what he'd do. I wanted to see him get at least a little bit annoyed. The man wasn't *human* the way he forgave."

"What happened?"

"I confessed the next morning, and gave him his present, a new razor and strop. I cried. The worst part was that he'd forgotten his own birthday, too. Said there was nothing to forgive me for. Oh!" Bertha put her hand to her mouth and seemed to be holding back a sob.

Eliza sat as still as possible and waited. She didn't knit. She barely breathed.

"That man loved me so hard I knew I'd never do half of what I should to deserve it. And that was the point. He said I never had to do a thing to make him love me. He just did. He just loved me." Bertha's voice broke. "Do you know what that's like?"

"I can't imagine," said Eliza, ignoring the image of Joshua's blue eyes that appeared in her mind.

"I wish that for you," said Bertha. "I wish that for every woman, but I know it doesn't happen for most, and for that I'm truly sorry. That man. The one you ran away from?"

"My husband."

"Did you . . ."

"I don't think I ever loved him at all." Eliza released a breath she didn't know she'd been holding.

"Why did you marry him?"

"He dared me to." She snorted. "What a ridiculous reason. The truth is I was trying to stay in one place – near my sister. I thought maybe if I married, I'd figure out how to stay. I ended up running again, though. I always do."

"But you told me, that first day in Tillie's, that you had a good reason to run."

Eliza imagined George's fist, rushing toward her. "A very good reason."

"That's being sensible, Eliza. That's a virtue, not a flaw. What else makes you want to run?"

Eliza thought hard before she answered. The knitting helped, giving her fingers something to grasp while she struggled to hold on to her flying thoughts. "Fear."

"Of what?"

"That I'll end up in the same place."

"As what?"

"As where I started."

Bertha asked gently, "And that was . . ."

"The orphanage. With my sister."

"Oh, you poor wee things. How long were you there?"

"We were there fifteen years. I was tall and gangly at every age, and Honey has a lazy eye. No one wanted us, and Sister Margaret Luke wouldn't let us be adopted separately. When I was seventeen, I got my first job. I rented a tiny apartment, and took Honey out of there. I worked three jobs to pay for us both to go to college."

"That doesn't sound like running to me."

The steady clicking of Bertha's needles soothed Eliza. "When I graduated, when I knew Honey was going to be okay, I left. I went to Europe and taught English in three different countries. I barely stayed in one place more than three months at a time."

"Sounds adventurous."

"It was cowardly. Every time I made an attachment, I'd leave. First chance I got. Out like a shot. *Dang* it." Another stitch dropped from her left needle as if it had a will of its own.

"Don't hold the needles so tightly. They need room to breathe, so they can dance. No, like this." Bertha scooted forward and adjusted Eliza's fingers. "Don't wrap the yarn around your finger like that – you'll cut off the circulation to it like farmers do with a lamb's tail. Don't want your finger dropping off, do we? Why doesn't Joshua run sheep?"

"What?"

"He should. He's got those cattle, but with that hilly land sheep would do better. Then you could have the wool."

"I'm not staying."

"Why not?"

"Because we . . . we're . . . I just work for him."

"Then why are your cheeks so flushed, my darling?"

Eliza scrubbed her face with her hands. "No reason."

"He's a good man. Doesn't talk much, but neither did Nathaniel."

Despite herself, Eliza blurted, "He talks all the *time*."

Bertha sat back with a look of satisfaction. "Oh, he does, does he?"

"Bertha! I'm not staying."

Bertha dropped the shawl into her lap and raised her hands. "Of course! You leave whenever you like, darlin'. Just say goodbye to me before you go, promise?"

"I promise."

"And remember, staying is sometimes the most exciting thing there is."

The words stayed, strung like soft yarn between them. Eliza felt their import, their weight, but couldn't respond.

"Now leave me, sweet girl. I've been looking forward to crying all day for weeks, and I've barely got started."

CHAPTER THIRTEEN

The next afternoon, while sawing the boards that would make a built-in bookcase for the parlor – Eliza's suggestion – she said to Joshua, "Bertha thinks you should get some sheep."

"Sheep, huh?" He watched as she fought the sawing. When he sawed, he made it look so easy. A few strong strokes and the boards broke perfectly, as though he'd scored them first. When Eliza sawed she had to grit her teeth and push all her energy into the back-and-forth motion, and the metal tip still only wiggled back and forth ineffectively. She stopped. Sweat from the sun behind her trickled down the small of her back. Briefly, she wondered how disheveled she must look right now.

"I can't do this while you're watching." Those butterflies, always present near Joshua, came fluttering back. If this kept up, she'd end up lopping off a finger or two.

"Don't push it so hard," he said. "Lean into the movement."

Eliza put the saw down on top of the half-cut wood. "You always say that, and I don't know what you mean."

He got closer. "Try again."

"No."

"Please?"

Grudgingly, she picked up the saw again. "If I damage myself, I'm holding you personally responsible."

"Noted." He stood behind her. "Now, see how your wrist is bending down at that angle?"

Eliza pushed as hard as she could, and the blade jerked away with a screech.

"You're using the wrong motion. Straighten your wrist so it aligns with your forearm, see?" He touched her then, his hand brushing her elbow, guiding her wrist into place. "Now, lean forward, with your weight behind your right hip – here."

Joshua's hand grazed her right side.

Eliza had always greatly disliked women who swooned, and thought they just needed to take more salt into their diets. Why, then, with a history of consuming all the salt she liked, did she feel as if her knees weren't going to hold her up much longer? With a deep breath, she leaned forward the way Joshua had told her to. It was a method of putting space between them, after all.

She cut through the board as if it were made of old lace.

"Oh!" Eliza placed the now-free saw on the sawhorse while stepping sideways. Away from him. To her great chagrin, she knew it wasn't the direction in which she really wanted to move.

"Good," Joshua said easily, as if he somehow possessed all the breath Eliza had lost. "Good job, you. Now, what's this about sheep?"

"Yarn," said Eliza stupidly. "Women want yarn."

Joshua pushed his cowboy hat back, tilting his face to the sun. It was only noon, but the stubble had grown in along his jawline, and Eliza had to push her hands into the pockets of her blue jeans to prevent her fingers from reaching toward him. What was wrong with her?

"Yarn. Huh. And you want yarn?"

"Um, I . . ." Why was he asking her that?

"Far as I know, yarn doesn't come right off the sheep like that, all clean and colored and spun."

She looked at her hands, now almost as callused as his. "Wouldn't it be fun to learn how to make it that way, though?"

He smiled. "You want me to spin wool?"

"I suppose not." She couldn't possibly voice what she was thinking – that she could learn. And that way, he wouldn't have to.

Joshua said, "It does sound fun. I could learn my way around a spinning wheel, I think. Just some gears, right?"

And there he went, surprising her again. He had to quit doing that – it wasn't good for her constitution. "More salt," she whispered to herself.

"Pardon?"

"Nothing."

CHAPTER FOURTEEN

Eliza woke to the sound of a bleat.

A *bleat.*

She rolled out of her cozy nest, shrugged out of her nightgown and into her jeans and pulled on her coat, freeing her hair from where it became bound at her collar.

As she clambered down the ladder, the barn door opened. Through the bright sunlight she felt, rather than saw, a commotion – a flurry of limbs and movement. She heard Joshua say something she couldn't understand, and then, quite clearly, she heard him swearing.

"Open that stall door!" he yelled.

Shocked, Eliza grabbed the door he had pointed at and yanked, just in time for two bolting sheep to run through it.

"Now shut it!"

She did.

Joshua whooped and grabbed her, swinging her up and around. "I didn't know what in tarnation I was doing! I don't know why I thought I could move those two sheep anywhere more than two feet by myself. Murphy had two dogs to help him, but I figured I'd work that out somehow." He stopped turning and released her, suddenly looking surprised she was in his arms at all. "Sorry."

He didn't have to be sorry. Eliza would happily have opened seventy-six more stalls before breakfast if he'd hold her like that again.

Slowly, she said, "You got sheep."

"Two! So we'll have babies!" His cheeks reddened. "I mean, they'll have babies. I mean, someday. They're both girls – ewes, I mean. You can't have a ram with them because—" Joshua's voice cracked.

"I understand," she said. She laughed to see him so flustered, two spots of color burning under his tanned cheekbones. "I think it's wonderful."

"You do?"

She nodded. "Yes."

"You really do?"

He stepped closer. He was asking her something else, something Eliza couldn't begin to – couldn't hope to – believe in.

Joshua took her hands, one in each of his. His skin felt rough and hardened next to hers, yet warm. Solid. Before she could stop herself, she moved her thumb across his palm, memorizing the placement of each callus. It was infinitely more intimate a moment than when he'd been swinging her around.

"Eliza," he started.

"No," Eliza said, pulling her hands away. "Don't."

"Why—"

"I need some paper." *Please don't ask.* She saw him swallow. *I need a divorce. I have to get a divorce.*

"Do you need a pen, too?" His low growl was almost a caress, sending an unforgivable shiver down her back.

"No." Eliza ducked her head. "I have one, and ink, too. But thank you."

In the barn's loft, using a small plank as a lap-desk, Eliza wrote:

George, I want a divorce. I'm not coming back, ever. You should be free to do as you wish, as should I. Please respond by return mail.

It was dangerous sending George her current address, but he'd need it at some point if they were to sever their marriage officially.

George was possessive, and proud. After she gave the letter to Flora, the postmistress in Cypress Hollow, Eliza dug her fingernails into her palms. What if George came looking for her? What if he demanded his truck back? She'd stolen it, after all. He had that right.

Good lord, it was his right to demand his *wife* back, too.

She heard the barn door slide shut far below her.

Over knitting at Tillie's a few weeks earlier, Bertha had told Eliza in a hushed voice that Joshua hadn't courted anyone since Lizzie Beckens ran off with Thomas Cain two years before. *Thomas teaches music. She never could see herself on a farm, always said so, too. Town girl. I never thought she broke Joshua's heart, though. He didn't have that wounded animal look behind his eyes. Besides, even though you share the same name, she was such a Lizzie. Good riddance, I say.*

What would Joshua do if George came to get her? Would he do anything at all?

CHAPTER FIFTEEN

Eliza got tired of watching for the mail every day and Joshua, it seemed, got tired of her doing so. One hot afternoon, out of nowhere, he said, "Let's take the afternoon off."

Surprised, she looked up from the tiling she was doing in the bathroom. Once the tiles were in, they could haul up the clawfoot tub, the one that was currently resting in the dirt outside. The one he'd asked her to choose from the Sears catalogue, saying, "I can't make this kind of decision – it's for a woman to make. Choose the fixtures, please, Eliza. You'd be doing me a huge favor."

Even though she wasn't staying, Eliza dreamed of taking one – just one – bath in that gorgeous beast of a tub before she left. Oh, to soak for an hour in warm water...

Now he was smiling at her in the dusty sunshine, but the skin at the corners of his eyes was tight. "Seriously. It's too hot to work up here."

Eliza pushed a sweaty lock of hair out of her eyes. "Do you want to work on the back porch instead?"

"No," he said, his voice almost impatient. "Let's go to the falls."

"Where?"

"Do you have a bathing suit?"

She nodded. It was still shoved into the pocket of her suitcase, just in case.

"Go get it."

Smythe Falls, it turned out, were just before Mills Bridge. They rattled there in Joshua's truck, Eliza holding on to the door handle as he took the road just a little too fast. He pulled up at the base of a narrow, steep trail.

"We're going hiking?"

"It's not far."

"Are you all right?" Eliza was becoming concerned. She could feel the tension pouring from him in waves. Maybe he was about to fire her? There wasn't that much more to do in the house. The job was almost over, the plumbing and plastering would complete it. How long could they keep working on it together? Another week? Maybe he was just going to get letting her go over with, do the rest of the work himself. He could finish it – including all the small details like painting and furnishing, things he'd conferred with her about – in four weeks, maybe three. Easily before fall brought colder weather.

He looked at her in surprise, as if he was seeing her properly for the first time all day. "Yeah. I'm sorry, Eliza. I just need to blow off some steam. Come on."

Joshua took the trail with powerful strides, almost running up the hillside. Eliza trotted behind him as fast as she could. It was gorgeous here, the foliage a lush, verdant green. Creeping ivy jostled with heavy ferns, creating dense underbrush beneath the sheltering live oak canopy that stretched above. It was cooler here than it had been at the ranch, and Eliza could feel the moisture in the air.

The base of the falls came into sight. The water crashed into a wide pool of green-blue water. Slick gray rocks shone in the sunshine, and a small rainbow formed in the mist.

"Oh," said Eliza. "This is the prettiest place I've ever been."

Joshua stopped and turned to face her. "I don't know why I haven't brought you here before."

Eliza shrugged. "We've been working." He was standing so close. She could have reached out and touched the chambray of his shirt if she'd wanted to, which, of course, she didn't . . .

"I'm an idiot."

She laughed lightly. "What? Of course you aren't. Let's swim."

"No, Eliza." He turned his body toward her. His voice was different. Lower. Rougher. "I'm such an idiot. And I'd like to apologize for my actions in advance. But if I don't do this, I'm going to lose my ever-lovin' mind."

"What do you—"

Joshua cupped her face in his hands – those strong, fine hands – and kissed her.

He kissed her like he'd been doing it for years, and as if he'd never get another chance. His mouth wasn't tentative. There was nothing shy about the kiss. He didn't ask her permission.

He took the kiss from her.

And God in heaven, Eliza gave it back. She kissed him hard. Wantonly. She shocked herself with the way she met his tongue as it stroked hers, first gently, and then with authority.

He tasted exactly as Eliza would have imagined, if she'd ever allowed herself to have this dream – of the mint toothpaste she'd seen at the outside well, of his morning coffee, and of something that was entirely him. She wanted to taste more, to taste him everywhere. His kiss was heady, coursing through her veins like whiskey. He pulled her flush against him, and his body was hard – so hard – in all the right places. Joshua groaned low in his throat, and just as Eliza clutched at his shirt to either keep herself standing or stop him from moving away – she couldn't tell which – he pulled back.

"Lord have mercy, woman." He pinched the bridge of his nose. "Eliza. I didn't know I would do that."

"Don't—" Eliza tried to catch her breath. She loved the look on his face, his cheeks ruddy, his lips still shining wet, his eyes so heated she thought they might melt.

"You're still married. I didn't mean to—" Joshua shoved both hands into his pockets, as if he couldn't trust himself not to touch her again.

To touch her again . . . Why couldn't he just do that? Where was the harm?

If Eliza were more like Josephine, she wouldn't have cared. She would have taken him by the hand and led him back to the truck. They'd have driven back to the ranch, and she'd have walked with him across the long yard, into the barn, and up into her aviary. There, in the bed he used to sleep in, they'd have made love.

She took a deep breath and touched her own lips. "I'll be divorced soon." *But you'll never want me then. A divorced woman.* She was already damaged goods. Used. Defective.

"I know. It's not—" He didn't finish the sentence, and Eliza was desperate to know how he would have. *It's not fair? It's not right? It's not possible?*

Without another word, he turned and walked to the edge of the pond. He tore off his shirt, and shucked off his jeans, leaving on only his shorts. Eliza's eyes widened at seeing his bare legs for the first time, which were as strong and muscled as his arms. He leaped forward with a whoop, splashing into the pond in a cannonball. He stayed under just long enough to worry her, coming up with another shout.

She wanted nothing more than to throw herself into the water and into his arms.

***

When Eliza was twenty-two, she taught English in Spain for six months. She made friends at the small university where she worked, and one of the other teachers introduced her to her cousin. Luíz had beautiful bronze eyes and full lips, and he'd danced with her for the first time in a moonlit square in Barcelona. There hadn't been any music in the square, the musicians having packed it in an hour earlier. Not even the drinkers were out anymore – it was so late that they'd all stumbled home and were happily snoring in their beds. The moon had long since plunged behind the hill, and the only light was from a gas lamp that flickered and hissed behind them.

Luíz had kissed her that night. Her first kiss. She'd always been too busy in school, too busy working, too busy making sure Honey was cared for to make time or space for a man in her life.

But the moment his lips met hers, something became clear – she was born to be kissed. Born to kiss. What a method of communicating! No wonder the human race went on, if people were drawn together like this.

Luíz was a fine man – a kind one. He took her home to meet his mother. He hoped, with every kiss, that Eliza was falling in love with him, and he was never shy about telling her so.

Eliza had known, though, that something wasn't quite right. When she stood next to him, she felt like a china figure, something that should be put safely out of harm's way. Luíz was a bull beside her, his hands gargantuan next to hers. When she placed her two hands on his cheeks, she couldn't span the full width of his strong face. His father, too, filled the church door with his height and breadth, and his mother lifted sacks of grain like Eliza lifted a stack of books. In his mother's house, Eliza felt as though she would be swept into the corner by his grandmother's efficient broom. Even when she spoke her loudest Spanish, carefully pronouncing her words as well as she could, her voice couldn't be heard over the friendly shouting in the packed kitchen. Her words went largely unnoticed, even by Luíz, who tried

valiantly to hear her. She didn't feel like constantly re-
peating herself, though, and when pressed she always
said, "*No es importa.*"

Luíz went so far as to buy her a ring. It, too, was
enormous, and didn't even fit her thumb. No diamond
for him, this ring was inset with a red ruby as big as her
pinkie nail, and she knew he must have spent his entire
savings on it, the money he'd been stockpiling to start
his own butcher shop. Holding his first finger as she
always did (as a child would do), she led him gently back
to the jewelry store. The jeweler, having seen this before,
handed back Luíz's money, less a "transfer" fee that Eliza
reimbursed into Luíz's coat pocket when he wasn't looking.

His love felt wonderful – warm, safe. She hoped what
she felt with him was a foreshadowing of something
stronger that could exist for her in the future, somewhere else.

The last time she'd seen Luíz was from the train's
open window. He'd stood on the platform in his second-
best jacket. He hadn't waved. He'd just watched her go,
his huge brown eyes swimming with tears that fell, soak-
ing his chest.

Sometimes Eliza liked to think of him. She knew that
a man such as he, one who loved so readily and hugely,
would have hurt, possibly deeply, for some time. Then,
someday, he would be in the marketplace buying something prosaic – almonds, or milk – and he would laugh,
his cheeks almost splitting with joy. Some fine young

woman would see him, and would want to be held in those arms, so strong they were meant for holding a woman as large as the sky. He would be happy, happiest with five or six solidly built children tumbling around his feet. Eliza liked to imagine him joyously roaring at them in a kitchen that was always too hot, always too crowded.

She was nothing but a skinny, pale passer-by. A fleeting moment in his life.

Maybe that's all she could ever be to anyone. She had been George's first marriage, the one that technically lasted three years but really only spanned six months of physical togetherness. She had been Honey's sister, as much as she could, as long as she was able. Honey would say, of course, that they were always sisters, but didn't sisters stay together? Live nearby? Hold each other through the bad times, and celebrate the good ones? She'd abandoned Honey so many times she was surprised whenever Honey seemed happy to see her again.

She was Joshua's employee. His itinerant worker.

Someday, Joshua's future wife would sit in Tillie's, knitting with Bertha, gossiping about the transient woman who had lived in Joshua's barn of all places. She would wonder, fleetingly, if there had ever been anything between Joshua and that strange woman, but Bertha would pooh-pooh any such worries. *Don't you worry about her, sugar. I taught her to knit, but I can barely remember her face. You're the one for Joshua. Eliza was just passing through. A drifter.* Eliza stood in the same spot Joshua had left her, watching as he swam, ducking under the falls and then back out again.

When he stood on this ground, his feet probably felt as rooted as the old oaks behind her.

She was a drifter. Adrift.

CHAPTER SIXTEEN

When Honey gave birth to Rosemarie, Eliza was with her in the hospital room while Honey's husband paced the narrow corridor outside. It was one of the most amazing things Eliza had ever seen, the moment when Honey took the brand new, very bald, tiny girl into her arms and held on as if she'd never let go. Honey said, fiercely, "I'll never let her out of my sight. I'll be with her, always."

Eliza had smiled and touched the baby's cheek. "What about when she gets married and moves away?"

"I'll pack myself in her suitcase and live under her bed."

Eliza laughed. "I'm sure her husband won't mind."

"Of course not. I'm her *mother*."

Neither of them said what they both knew they were thinking – that their mother had let them go. Had given them away. Their mother was the reason they'd ended up in the orphanage, and Eliza's ferocity at taking care of Honey had assured they stayed there.

Sister Margaret Luke, at least, had been kind to them. Others were swift with the rod for the smallest fault, but Sister Margaret Luke was a woman who'd become a nun so she could nurture more children than she would have naturally. But all the love one woman could give didn't spread far enough over the more than forty children who routinely filled the rooms of the orphanage. The other sisters did the best they could, but the emphasis in the home was always on religion and saving the children's souls, rather than making them feel loved.

Sister Margaret Luke had once given Eliza a thin golden necklace. It had a charm in the shape of a star and a clasp that was partially broken – the tooth of it broken off, lost somewhere along the way. Sister had shown her how to tie the two ends together so that it stayed securely around her neck.

Eliza, only ten at the time, had been lost for words. She'd touched it, memorizing the feel of the star against her fingertips so that if it was taken away from her in the future, she'd always know the shape of it by heart. "You're *giving* this to me?"

Sister had touched her cheek, lightly. "You're a special one, Eliza."

"Me?" Eliza felt astonishment, as sharp as the star around her neck's points.

"You love so hard, little one. You take such good care of Honey that you don't let anyone else near her."

Of course – Eliza and Honey were a family. They didn't *need* anyone else. Eliza knew that in her heart.

But it felt so good to drink in the look Sister was giving her. It was the look she'd seen mothers give their real children when they visited the orphanage. Parents only had two different reasons for bringing their children to the Home – either they were allowing them to assist with picking the new child they'd take home, or they were on a warning mission. *Keep acting that way, and you'll end up here with these poor children. We'll leave you here,* they hissed.

Eliza avoided both kinds of parents like she avoided the cod liver oil Sister Jude pressed on them at night-time. During viewing, she fled to the back orchard, dragging Honey with her. Once there, sheltered under a stunted apple tree, she would tell Honey stories, making up tales of dragons and princesses and lands of great riches. In every story, there was always a mother who loved her child unconditionally, a mother who sacrificed all to keep her children safe. Eliza made sure the sisters only returned long after the interlopers were gone.

When Honey took Rosemarie into her arms that first time, Eliza saw the embodiment of that so-often verbalized wish. Here was the princess mother, with her charmed, beloved child.

Honey no longer needed Eliza.

It was good, and right and natural. It was for the best. And yet that single moment broke Eliza's heart.

***

When Joshua finished his swim, he got out and draped himself across a sunny rock, his arm over his eyes. "You should go in. There's a hot spring that flows into the pool, and it's warm on this side."

Eliza, who'd been standing, still stunned, under an oak tree, took the opportunity of his eyes being closed to strip down to her suit. The fabric was black, thick and demure, but she still felt almost naked. She ran as fast as she could into the water (which wasn't warm – he was a liar. It was freezing).

"Water's warmer over this way," he said without opening his eyes.

But the warm water was on the side closest to where he was lying. She chose to stick to the cold water, just as she then chose to dry herself on a far rock and dress again, quickly, before he stood and pulled on his own clothes. They walked back to the truck and drove back to the ranch, and not a word passed between them. For the first time, Eliza felt a fervent wish that she had her knitting with her. Instead, she knitted air, hoping Joshua wouldn't notice the small motions of her fingers.

Joshua parked in front of the barn. He mumbled something about bringing the sheep in and Eliza didn't bother answering. Neither of them was able to say the words they wanted to. Everything felt wrong. Crimped, somehow pinched.

She walked farther up the drive and through the new front door into the house they'd made together – for that's what it was now, a real house with framed walls and finished ceilings and floors. These last jobs they were doing within the walls, the electricity and the plumbing, soon they'd be covered by plaster and wallpaper, and all the work they'd done in the heart of the house, inside its very guts, would be covered up.

As Eliza walked through the kitchen, she thought, as she so often did, about the woman who would eventually make this room her own. Would she love the way the light slid lazily across the counters as much as Eliza did? Would she appreciate the stove, brushed iron and burnished steel, that Eliza had chosen? Would she know that Joshua had thought that there only needed to be one set of cabinets, and hadn't even considered lining the back wall with more? Would she like that Eliza had removed the doors on the sideboard Joshua bought, creating an open bookcase for cookbooks and novels that needed to be read in the kitchen? Would Joshua ever tell her that he hadn't even thought of including a pantry, that Eliza had rocked back on her heels and laughed when he'd asked her why a pantry was important, if they kept food in the cupboards and refrigerator?

She pulled open the drawer nearest the sink. A pile of cheery blue gingham tea-towels rested inside, already folded and ready for use. She'd bought the linen at the mercantile, and trimmed the tea-towels herself, sewing the hems at night when she needed a break from her knitting. She ran her fingertips across them. The linen would get softer every time it was washed.

Eliza wouldn't feel them softening.

Tonight, she'd pack. At dawn – no, before dawn, before Joshua rose – she'd leave. She could almost feel the suitcase's handle under her fingers. She slipped one (just one) tea-towel out of the drawer. She'd wrap it around her knitting, to keep it safe.

CHAPTER SEVENTEEN

Honey didn't ask a single question.

Eliza arrived in the early evening. San Diego felt the same, warm air mixed with a pleasant humidity. Everywhere smelled like jasmine. Honey put Eliza's suitcase on the twin bed in the spare room, and then steered her out to the backyard where Rosemarie was playing on a swing set her father had built her.

"Push me, Aunt Eliza!" As though Eliza hadn't been away for months.

Honey brought out two cups of tea, one already doctored, sweet and light, just as Eliza liked it.

"Honey," Eliza started.

Honey shook her head. "You don't have to tell me anything you don't want to."

"I'm sorry I didn't write more."

"At least you told me you were safe."

"I didn't want you to have to lie if George came asking where I was."

"He stopped coming after a month."

Eliza said, "I'm sorry you had to talk to him."

"I'm sorry you had to marry him."

Eliza nodded. "That's fair."

"You're different."

Eliza took a sip of her still-too-hot tea and watched Rosemarie's legs kick toward the sky on the swings. "How?"

"You seem like a different person."

"I've only been here for ten minutes."

"It's obvious, though." Honey tilted her head and directly stared at her. "Oh!"

"What?"

"You're in love."

Eliza swatted the air. "Stop it."

"Like, really in love. The way you never were with George."

"How could you possibly see something like that by just looking at me?" Eliza reached into her bag and pulled out her scarf.

"It's written all over your face. You're still there, with him. Wherever that is."

Eliza took a deep breath and tried to soak in everything around her – Honey's pink chrysanthemums, Rosemarie's white nighties slapping in the light breeze on the clothesline that ran along the fence, the bluest sky above, not a hint of the fog that perpetually wreathed the marina in Cypress Hollow, far away, hours and hours up the coast . . .

Her words came in a rush. "It took everything I could to leave. I woke an hour before dawn, before he could possibly be awake. I'd already packed everything, and I slept in my clothes. I rolled the truck down the driveway and didn't start it until I was halfway down. But in my rear-view mirror, I saw a light go on in the house. We'd just put in the electricity, and he's been staying in there, in the room that will be his bedroom some day. He put down a straw pallet. But I stayed in the barn, because it was warm, and cozy, and because I'd hear him down below me, feeding the animals before I woke every morning. And because if I stayed in the house, he'd never live down the gossip. I saw that light go on, and I knew . . ."

"What?" Honey's voice was soft.

"That he knew I was leaving." Suddenly the thought of Joshua hurting in any way was completely intolerable to her.

"Why did you?"

"Because I had to."

"But why?"

"Because I'm not good enough."

"Bullshit."

Eliza had never heard Honey swear, not in her whole life, and it shocked her.

Honey cast a quick glance at Rosemarie to make sure she was still swinging, safely out of earshot. "You're good enough for any man."

"I'm married."

"In your letter you said you'd asked George for a divorce."

"That he'll have to pursue. Or I can go to Nevada, but that takes money, which I don't have. Either way, it requires contacting him." She sighed heavily. "I have to give him his truck back, too."

"Whatever it takes. You'll do it. Then you'll be divorced."

"Joshua can't marry" – even the word hurt to say – "a divorced woman. He's too good for that." That was the hardest part – she *wasn't* good enough for him. But who, then, was? Who would make a perfect wife for the man of her dreams? She couldn't bear to think about it.

"Joshua. That's a good, strong name. What's he like?"

Could she talk about him without breaking? "He's tall. Blue eyes so bright they look like sea glass."

"More, please."

"He's good." Wasn't that the most important part? "He's kind."

"So he's like you."

Eliza's heart broke again and she felt her eyes fill with tears. "I don't stay. You know that. Joshua needs someone he can trust. He deserves the best kind of woman." She finished the row and looked up. "Do you mind if I go to bed?"

"It's four o'clock—" Honey seemed to catch herself. "Of course you can. I'll wake you for supper. We'll be quiet."

They weren't, though. Rosemarie, naturally rambunctious, had been born loud. And Eliza was glad. She lay in the twin bed, under the thin red and blue quilt Honey had sewn, and listened to her niece bounce and sing and run. She kept her eyes wide open, fixed on the picture that hung on the wall – a small landscape of a green hill. Just over the ridge, Eliza imagined, was a white house with a wraparound porch. She felt hollow with grief. A hummingbird without a heart.

Every time she closed her eyes, she saw Joshua.

She'd just stay awake then. Forever, if she had to.

CHAPTER EIGHTEEN

Eventually, somehow, Eliza slept. As she woke, her eyes still shut, she listened for the sound of the sheep rustling below, the sliding screech of the barn door.

Then she remembered where she was, and her heart ached once more.

It was dark. She pushed aside the sheer curtain and looked out. A single streetlight shone – its light clearly illuminating the spot in front of the house where she'd parked the truck.

Which wasn't there.

George. He must have come to the house. He'd seen the truck and taken it back. Had he confronted Honey? Was Rosemarie okay? As she pulled on her shoes, her hands shook. She couldn't move quickly enough – it felt like she was in a nightmare.

The handle of the door stuck in the jamb – it always had. She yanked it with all her strength, and then ran down the short hallway.

"Honey! Where are you?" Eliza raced into the kitchen, where Honey sat piecing a puzzle together with Rose-marie. Bob stood at the stove, stirring something that smelled like stew.

Honey calmly looked up at her and said, "There's someone waiting for you in the sitting room."

"Oh no!" The air left Eliza's lungs, and she clenched her hands into fists. "I'm sorry. I'm sorry about George. I'll handle him – somehow. I promise."

Honey didn't look worried. She placed a piece at the edge of the board and waved her hand. "Go. See."

"I'm sorry. I'm so sorry about this . . ." Eliza backed out of the kitchen.

The small sitting room was dark, a light glow coming through the sheers that covered the windows. Silhouetted against the curtain was a man, his back to the room.

For one brief second, she imagined it was Joshua standing there – Joshua who'd come for her, and not George. They were almost the same height – she'd never noticed that. George's shoulders were as wide as Joshua's, too. She hadn't remembered that. In her mind, Joshua was so much bigger. So much more.

She pushed the fear back. "George," she said.

The man turned.

It was Joshua.

"Oh," she breathed. Her knees literally gave out, and she sat on the sofa. Eliza, who'd never fainted, not once, noticed small silver sparkles dancing at the edge of her vision. "You're here." She was confused, so confused. "How on earth did you find me?"

"I bribed Flora at the post office to give me your sister's address." He crossed the room to stand in front of her.

So close that she could reach out and touch him. "But—"

"Not with money. Although I'd have tried that, if I'd thought it would work. I gave her a sheep."

"What?"

"That bossy ewe, the one you don't like."

It was true, that sheep and Eliza had never seen eye to eye.

"But who's watching the ranch?"

"Zane Wegman's helping me out. I'm paying his son Pete to do the chores for as long as I'm gone."

Faintly, Eliza said, "I'm sure he'll do fine overnight. Pete's a good boy."

"He'll do fine no matter how long it takes."

"How long . . . what takes?"

Joshua pointed to the doorway, where a suitcase, large and dark, sat.

Nothing was making sense to Eliza. "I don't understand."

"I left the ranch."

"You don't leave the ranch."

He shrugged. Then he pulled Honey's blue chair forward with his foot and sat, facing her. "I never thought I would. I thought it was home."

"It is your home."

"You're my home."

"Oh . . ." Eliza dug her fingers into the scratchy sofa cover. "But—"

Joshua interrupted her. "There's nothing for me there if you're not there too."

"You wanted to die there."

"It's just some old dirt."

"It's your dirt." She couldn't stay. She never stayed. She couldn't let herself break Joshua's heart, the way hers was already splitting into tiny pieces.

"Where are you going next?" he asked. His eyes held hers, wouldn't let her go.

"I don't know."

"May I come with you?"

She laughed. This was insanity. "You don't travel."

"I do now – if you'll let me. I'll go anywhere with you." He glanced over his shoulder. "I didn't even own a suitcase but I bought that one. Figured I'd need it, to keep up with you."

Eliza stood and paced back and forth with quick, short steps, unable to keep from moving. "I'm married. Oh, Jesus. His truck. George's truck is gone—"

"I returned it to him."

She frowned. "What?"

"Honey told me where he lived, and Bob followed me over."

"You talked to *George*?"

Joshua stood, too. He looked down at his hand as he flexed it. Eliza could see that his knuckles were bruised. "Talk is not quite what I'd call it."

"You *hit* him?"

"Only after he tried to hit me first. Not much of a fighter, that one. He'll give you the divorce, by the way. He'll start the paperwork tomorrow."

She could feel the draw of his being so close – it was as if he was a magnet and she was iron. He kept still, though. He didn't move a muscle, just kept those glorious eyes on hers. Eliza's heart pounded in her ears.

She took Joshua's hand in hers and gently, so gently, kissed his knuckles. "Where would we go?"

"Wherever you want to go, my love."

My love.

"Paris?" She pressed another kiss to his thumb.

"*Oui,*" he said.

"China?"

"I don't know how to say yes in Chinese, but if I did, I'd say it." His words were light, but his hand was shaking in hers.

"What if I wanted to go to Mongolia?"

"I'd buy a better coat and make sure you had the warmest gloves I could find."

Something inside Eliza slid into place. As if, for the very first time, she knew what she wanted. What she needed.

"What if I wanted to go home?"

Joshua blinked. "What?"

"To the ranch."

"You would . . ." He didn't complete the thought.

Eliza couldn't complete it, either. She could only nod.

Joshua whooped, once, his whole face splitting into a grin that was the brightest, happiest thing Eliza had ever seen in her whole life. He pulled her into his arms, but she was already there. "I built it for you, you know."

She laughed, an unfamiliar joy building in her chest. "You didn't know me."

"I did. As soon as I met you, I knew who the house was for. Just didn't know if you'd ever have me. If you'd stay. I looked for that damned truck first thing every morning, praying you had stayed one more day." Joshua lifted her hand to his mouth. "I don't mind travelling, Eliza. I don't mind anything. As long as you're with me."

"Take me home, please."

Eliza kissed him then. He kissed her back, his lips firm and warm. She felt as if she'd kissed him a million times, and it felt like the first time. She felt tears on her cheek. She wasn't sure whose they were, and it didn't matter. "I'm not going anywhere without you."

EPILOGUE

Every year, on their anniversary, Joshua packed two suitcases. Hers he filled with clothes, her favorite knitting needles, and whatever knitting pattern she was working on at the time. In his, he put a light jacket and a heavier one. "Just in case," he said. Before they went to sleep, he would show her where they were, placed carefully under the bed.

"We can go," he said every year. "I'm always ready."

As though Eliza would ever leave the ranch, the animals she loved, the dirt her toes dug into as she hung the washing on the line. As though Eliza didn't feel the same way about the sun that sank over the western hill, into the ocean hidden behind it.

And every year, on their anniversary, after Joshua had fallen asleep, Eliza got up quietly and unpacked their suitcases, returning the clothes to their drawers, putting away her knitting needles and pattern. She crawled back in bed, and Joshua's arms tightened around her.

Every year, she said in his ear, "I'll be here in the morning."

He always said the same thing. "That's fine, then. That's the finest thing in the world."

ABOUT THE AUTHOR

Rachael Herron is the internationally bestselling author of the Cypress Hollow series (HarperCollins/Random House Australia) and of the memoir, A Life in Stitches (Chronicle). Her newest novel, Pack Up The Moon, will be available in March 2014 from Penguin (USA) and Random House Australia (NZ/AUST). Rachael received her MFA in writing from Mills College and is a 911 fire/medical dispatcher when she's not scribbling. She lives with her wife, Lala, in Oakland, California, where they have more animals and instruments than are probably advisable. Rachael is struggling to learn the accordion and can probably play along with you on the ukulele. She's a New Zealander as well as an American. She's been known to knit.

Website: Yarnagogo.com
Email: yarnagogo@gmail.com
Twitter: @rachaelherron

CPSIA information can be obtained
at www.ICGtesting.com
Printed in the USA
LVHW080031280720
661693LV00013B/735